A Jar of Pickles and a Pinch of Justice

Stories from India

Chitra Soundar

illustrated by Uma Krishnaswamy

To my mum, for her inspiration
and unconditional support
C.S.

Thanks, Jacky, two times lucky!
U.K.

First published 2016 by Walker Books Ltd
87 Vauxhall Walk, London SE11 5HJ

2 4 6 8 10 9 7 5 3 1

Text © 2016 Chitra Soundararajan
Illustrations © 2016 Uma Krishnaswamy

The right of Chitra Soundararajan and Uma Krishnaswamy to be
identified as author and illustrator respectively of this work
has been asserted by them in accordance with the Copyright,
Designs and Patents Act 1988

This book has been typeset in StempelSchneidler

Printed in Great Britain by Clays Ltd, St Ives plc

British Library Cataloguing in Publication Data:
a catalogue record for this book is available from the British Library

ISBN 978-1-4063-6467-5

www.walker.co.uk

Contents

All's Well with Mango Pickles
7

**Freezing Lakes
and Missing Crows**
28

What's Fair?
56

Grey Elephants and Five Fools
73

All's Well with Mango Pickles

Long ago in a faraway land, King Bheema ruled a small kingdom surrounded by the magnificent hills of Himtuk. He was a kind and just ruler. He lived with his wife and his son, Prince Veera.

Prince Veera studied many subjects: the arts, mathematics,

7

science, economics and languages, including Persian, Latin and Mandarin.

Prince Veera's best friend, Suku, was not a royal. Suku had won the king's scholarship to study with the prince. He matched Veera's academic abilities and outdoor activities. Often the two boys competed in sports, such as wrestling, archery and horse riding. When classes were over for the day, Prince Veera and Suku would wander through the markets and play in the mangrove.

The previous summer, King Bheema had been unwell. Prince Veera and Suku offered to help out with his duties, and the king had allowed them to set up a court in the palace courtyard. There the boys listened to people's problems and solved petty disagreements.

Now the hot summer months were here once again.

"With no work to do on the farm and no classes," said Suku, "I'm bored."

"Maybe we can ask Father to invite us to the dance performances in the palace," suggested Prince Veera.

"Please don't," said Suku. "I can't sit in one place with a smile on my face for hours on end."

"That's my future you're describing!" said Veera. "What would you rather do instead?"

"We could set up court," Suku replied.

Prince Veera's eyes twinkled. "What a good idea," he said with a big grin. "Let's ask Father before he leaves for his hunting trip," he added, pulling Suku through the corridors.

As they entered the royal chambers they found the king's room in a flurry. Attendants were packing bags, clothes were strewn everywhere and King Bheema was pacing the floor.

"Is something wrong?" asked Suku.

"Packing is always traumatic," explained Veera.

"I can't find my hunting knife," said King Bheema, exasperated.

"It should be where you left it," said the queen from behind a cupboard. She, too, was looking for something.

"That's not very helpful," said the king. "Where did I leave it?"

Veera chuckled. His parents had the same conversation every time one of them left town.

"Did you two want something?" the king asked the boys.

"While you're away hunting," said Prince Veera, "we wondered if we could run the court in the courtyard."

"This boy is after my throne, I tell you," said King Bheema, smiling. "You may run the court as long as you don't bite off more than you can chew."

"We never do," said Prince Veera. "Thank you, Father. I wish you good fortune on your hunt."

"May the *vandevata,* the forest nymphs, help you along the way," wished Suku.

As they left, a loud whoop came from the room. The king must have found his hunting knife after all. The two boys rushed out to get ready for court the following day.

Next morning, a long queue of people waited outside the palace to meet the king. When they found out that he was away, many of them were disappointed.

"Prince Veera is happy to listen to your problems," announced the guard.

Some people left, but many stayed to meet with the prince. They had heard wonderful things about his court.

Prince Veera summoned the first case. Two neighbours, Gopu and Dhanu, had come with a unique problem. Gopu had an old well in his overgrown garden, which he never used. Dhanu wanted to buy the well. A price was agreed and a document was drawn up: *I hereby sell just my well, situated behind my house, to Dhanu, my neighbour, for ten silver coins.*

The two men signed the document and Dhanu was happy to acquire the well in time for the summer.

"So what's the problem?" asked Suku. "You sold him the well, he bought the well, so all's well."

Prince Veera smiled at Suku's bad joke.

But he couldn't figure out the cause of their disagreement either.

"I sold only the well, Your Majesty," said Gopu. "Not the water. So whenever Dhanu draws water from the well, he has to pay me half a silver."

Suku's jaw dropped open. Whoever heard of selling a well and charging for the water? Veera looked at Suku and raised his eyebrows.

"What do you say to that, Dhanu?" asked Prince Veera.

"Why would I buy just the well, Your Majesty?" asked Dhanu. "I need water for my garden during the summer months. But he wouldn't let me draw water from my own well unless I paid him half a silver."

"But you signed the document," said Gopu, waving a scroll in front of Dhanu. "It clearly says *'just my well'*."

Suku reached for the scroll. What Gopu said was true. This was a tricky problem! Veera wanted to talk it over with Suku. They went to the garden for a walk.

"Why would someone buy a well and not the water?" asked Veera.

"If the well was empty, he could store his pots and pans in it," suggested Suku.

"Or maybe he has relatives coming and they need room to stay," said Veera.

"Next time you come to stay," said Suku,

14

"I'll ask them to prepare the well!"

"I'm sure you would join me too," said Veera. "And maybe the well could be used as a hiding place." He was thinking about the hiding place his grandfather had made many years ago to escape from his enemies.

"The only trouble is," said Suku, "this well is not empty."

That's when Veera had an idea. "Come on, let's go," he said. "I know what to do."

"I've reached a decision," Prince Veera said, taking his seat in the courtyard.

Everyone was quiet. They wanted to know how the prince would solve this tricky case.

"According to the document, Dhanu bought only the well," said Prince Veera, "and not the water. Indeed, he should pay half a silver every time he draws water."

Gopu was overjoyed. The prince was very astute, he thought.

"But," Prince Veera continued, "he may have bought the well so that he could use it to store his belongings. Or perhaps he wants to live in the well."

Everyone was confused.

"As soon as the well was sold," explained Prince Veera, "Gopu should have removed the water."

"But, Your Majesty—" said Gopu.

"Shh!" warned Suku. Prince Veera wasn't finished.

"Gopu should take the water out of the well immediately or he should pay rent for storing the water in Dhanu's well."

Dhanu beamed. The prince was indeed wise and just, he thought.

Gopu hung his head in shame. The prince had outwitted him with his own trick. Gopu agreed not to charge Dhanu for the water lest he should be forced to pay for keeping the water in the well. The document was amended and the prince warned Gopu not to try such a trick again.

"That was a bit complicated," said Veera.

"It's water under the bridge now." Suku giggled.

"Seems like neighbours are not very nice to each other in our kingdom," observed Veera.

"That's why I live far away from the palace," said Suku. "You might not be a good neighbour."

Prince Veera chuckled. But he soon stopped, because the next man who came in was crying.

"Please," said Prince Veera. "Tell me your grievance."

17

"My name is Kasi, Your Majesty," said the man. "And I live next door to a man named Pawan."

"Are you crying because your name is Kasi or because you live next door to Pawan?" asked Suku.

"Neither," said Kasi. "I am crying because Pawan stole all my precious belongings." It seemed that neighbourly feuds were not over for the day.

"We'll be the judges of that," said Suku. "Please state your case."

"My mother passed away a year ago," said Kasi. "I had to go to the holy city of Varanasi to perform her death ceremony."

Varanasi was a long way away. It took months to get there, even on horseback.

"Did the ceremony complete to your satisfaction?" asked Suku.

"Yes, it did," replied Kasi. "But before I left for Varanasi, I handed over a jar of pickles to my neighbour, Pawan, for safekeeping."

"It is important to keep pickles safe," said Prince Veera. He loved the tender mango pickles that Suku's mother made for him. He hid the jars in the royal kitchens so that he could eat the pickles all year.

"Actually, the jar didn't have any pickles in it," said Kasi. "I filled it with all my precious belongings – my gold ring, gold chain, silver coins and even some rubies that had belonged to my mother."

"That's quite clever," said Suku. "So what is the problem?"

"I didn't tell my neighbour that it was filled with valuables. He thought it was filled with pickles."

"Then what happened?" asked Veera. Thinking of pickles had made his mouth water.

"When I came back yesterday and asked for the jar," said Kasi, "Pawan returned my jar filled with pickles. My gold and silver and rubies were gone."

"Lemon or mango?" asked Veera.

Suku nudged Veera. Was that even important?

"It was filled with tender mango pickles," said Kasi. He started to cry again.

Every story had two sides. Prince Veera and Suku wanted to hear what Pawan had to say. Pawan was summoned to the court, but when he came before the prince, he didn't look worried.

"At your service, Your Majesty," he said.

"Your neighbour, Kasi, has lodged a complaint," said Suku. "He claims that you stole his gold and silver."

"And rubies," added Prince Veera.

"That's totally untrue," said Pawan. "I didn't steal his gold, silver or rubies."

"Can you prove that?" asked Veera.

 "Kasi gave me the jar for safekeeping before he left on his travels," said Pawan. "He repeatedly said that the jar contained tender mango pickles made by his mum before she died. He wanted me to keep it safe until he returned."

Veera and Suku turned to look at Kasi, who was still crying.

"When Kasi came back yesterday, I returned his jar of pickles," Pawan continued. "You can ask him what was in the jar."

"The jar was filled with tender mango pickles, Your Majesty," said Kasi.

"He gave me pickles and he got back pickles," said Pawan. "I never stole any gold or silver or rubies."

Prince Veera was confused. Yet another

21

case that looked straightforward but wasn't. Was Kasi lying about the precious stones and silver and gold inside the jar or had Pawan stolen everything and filled the jar with pickles?

It was almost lunchtime and Veera was hungry. All this talk of pickles was making him even hungrier.

"Let's finish this later," said Veera. "I need to think about it a little longer."

While the prince and his friend went to the royal dining hall, all the people waiting to see Veera were served lunch in the courtyard.

As they walked Veera said, "I don't know who is lying."

"Maybe instead of eating here we should go to my house for lunch," Suku suggested. "My mother knows everything about pickles."

"That's the best idea you've had all day!"

said Prince Veera. He loved eating at Suku's
house. Suku's mother was a wonderful cook.
That day, she served them freshly made
bread with spinach, potatoes and lentils, and
some fresh fish too.

"How about some tender mango pickles
to go with the fish?" she asked.

"Absolutely," chimed the boys in unison.

Veera bit into the fried fish and took a bite
out of the tender pickled mango. Suku took
a mouthful of rice mixed with the lentils,
potatoes and fish.

"Eat slowly," warned Suku's mother.

"It's so good, we can't wait between
mouthfuls," said Veera.

23

"Tell me about your latest case," said Suku's mother. So they did.

Afterwards, she said, "I don't know anything about justice, dear Veera. But I know something about pickles."

Suku's mother presented them with two cups of tender mango pickles.

"This one, on the right," she said, "was made this time last year."

Suku and Veera touched the mango pieces. They were shrunken and wrinkly. Suku bit into a piece. It was very chewy and salty.

"This one, on the left," she said, "the one you had for lunch today, was made last week. The mangoes were fresh from the trees and soaked two days after being picked."

These pieces were bright green, without wrinkles. Veera bit into one. *Crunch!* The pickle was crunchy and the salt had not yet soaked into it.

Veera and Suku made their way back in silence. They were both busy thinking. The court was ready for them when they reached the palace. Before they entered, Suku said, "Are you thinking what I'm thinking?"

"Maybe," said Veera. "Are you thinking about crunchy pickles?"

"Maybe!"

As soon as Veera settled into his seat he said to Pawan, "I want to sample the pickles in the jar."

The guard placed the jar in front of the boys. The mango pieces were sloshing in the salt and chilly water. Suku took out two pieces of mango with a ladle.

The boys picked up one tender mango each and turned it around like they were looking at diamonds.

"Green!"

"Not wrinkly at all!"

"Let's try it," said Veera, and he bit into the piece. Suku did the same.

Crunch!

The mangoes were still fresh, like the ones they had eaten for lunch. These couldn't have been mangoes from last season. That meant Pawan had removed the contents of the jar and filled it with mangoes picked this season.

Pawan trembled as Veera glared at him. "You cheated your neighbour and stole his property," said Veera.

"And you thought we didn't know about pickles," said Suku.

Prince Veera confiscated all the stolen gold, silver and rubies and returned them to Kasi. Pawan was asked to work in the kitchens, making pickles for the rest of the season.

Kasi returned home, delighted that he had taken his case to the prince.

Prince Veera had one more thing to do: he talked to his father's minister and recommended that the palace organize a place of safekeeping, so that when people went away on long trips, they didn't have to worry about cheats and burglars. Something good for all the people would come out of something bad.

"This is an excellent idea!" said the minister. "You're surely taking after your father."

"Like mango, like pickle," said Suku. "That's what my mother always says."

Freezing Lakes
and Missing Crows

Prince Veera enjoyed running the court with
Suku in the king's absence, even if they
had to run it in the courtyard. He and Suku
always had a good time. But after a week
of listening to people complaining about
friends, families and neighbours, the boys
wanted a break.

"Let's go to the riverbank," said Suku. "We
could jump into the water and catch fish."

"That sounds perfect," said Veera.

"And then we could go to the market and buy some palm fruits."

But just as they were changing out of their formal court attire they heard news that King Bheema was on his way back home with a special guest. A welcome party was preparing to receive the king at the edge of the forest, where he was camping that night.

"The river will still be there tomorrow," said Veera. "Let's go and meet Father."

So the boys set off with the king's entourage. They took lots of food, fresh water and juice, and a band to play music.

The welcome party reached the king's camp by dusk. The king was overjoyed that Veera and Suku had come too. He was keen to hear about their week running their own court.

"Who is your guest, Father?" asked Veera.

"Do you want to meet him now?" asked the king. "I thought it could wait until morning."

"I'm curious," said Veera.

"Don't say I didn't warn you," said King Bheema, and he sent word to the other tent.

Within a few minutes, the king and the two boys were invited there.

Veera gulped when he saw who was inside.

"Uncle, you remember Veera," said King Bheema.

"Welcome, Grand-uncle" said Prince Veera. "Are you passing through?"

"I've not visited my dear nephew in a long while," said Raja Apoorva, "and I have some family matters to discuss too."

Oh no, thought Suku. This was the infamous uncle who handed out harsh punishments. The one who had never liked King Bheema or Prince Veera much. The palace walls were filled with gossip about Raja Apoorva.

Suku tried to blend in with the tent cloth. When he was introduced, Raja Apoorva just raised his right eyebrow as if to let King Bheema know that Veera was not keeping good company.

That night, after dinner, everyone sat outside their tents and chatted under the full moon.

"So what have you been up to?" Raja Apoorva asked Veera. "Surely you haven't been busy studying during the hot summer weeks?"

"We were running a court," said Prince Veera.

"What?" Raja Apoorva was surprised. Princes went on holidays in the hills during the summer.

As King Bheema proudly talked about the court cases from the previous year and how Veera had been courageous and just, Raja Apoorva shook his head.

"The prince is too young to listen to cases and bring justice to your people," he said.

"I have help," said Prince Veera. "Suku is very clever and knows about a lot of things."

Raja Apoorva grunted and ignored Suku completely.

The next morning, as the hunting party set off towards home, Raja Apoorva lagged behind, deep in thought. He had to show his nephew that the boys were not as clever as they thought and that a little knowledge was very dangerous.

By then the king and his group had reached the city. People stood on either side of the road to welcome him. The square got busier and busier as more people arrived. The king stopped to talk to a few people. Veera mingled too.

"Caw-caw!" the crows crowed, and the people said, "The crows are signalling the arrival of our royal guests."

This was a legend they had.

"Isn't that wonderful?" asked King Bheema. "Even the crows are happy that you're here. Indeed, your visit was long overdue."

"I've got a headache," said Raja Apoorva.

"Can you get someone to shoo the crows away, please?"

King Bheema sighed. He had been hoping to reach the palace without incident.

"They live here too," said King Bheema. "Don't you remember the ancient stories? The crows have lived in our kingdom for centuries."

"Are you the king of the people or the crows?" asked Raja Apoorva. "In my kingdom, we culled all the frogs that croaked at night and all the crows that dirtied my beautiful bronze statues throughout the city."

"What's a little white decoration?" said King Bheema, trying to bring some humour into the conversation.

But Raja Apoorva wasn't listening.

"Maybe in honour of my visit," said Raja Apoorva, "you should cull all the crows."

Suku overheard this comment and bristled with anger. Whoever thought of culling birds and animals that lived in peace? They were as much a part of the city as the people. All night he had been angry about how Raja Apoorva had ignored him or smirked at him. Now the visiting king was insulting King Bheema too.

King Bheema signalled the guards to guide the procession to the palace. It wasn't the time or the place to have an argument, especially with Raja Apoorva.

That evening, as the kings strolled in the garden, Veera and Suku joined them. A gentle breeze brought respite from the still-hot sun.

"Caw-caw!"

The harsh screech of the crows irritated Raja Apoorva again. "I told you," he said. "You've far too many crows in the capital and they disturb the royal peace. Even if you don't want to cull all of them, you should cull at least some."

"How many is far too many?" asked Prince Veera. Crows and sparrows were part of the gardens. Who could think of them as a disturbance?

He couldn't imagine a world without birds, butterflies, frogs and fireflies.

"How many do you have in the capital?" asked Raja Apoorva.

He was sure that the prince wouldn't be able to answer the question.

Veera blinked. "I don't know," he said. "With all due respect, Your Majesty, neither do you."

"Why don't you count the crows in the capital?" said Raja Apoorva. "Then we can have an informed debate."

Prince Veera knew this was a trap. The king was trying to make a fool out of him. Whoever heard of counting crows?

36

Sensing Veera's hesitation, Raja Apoorva chuckled. "I knew you would accept defeat at the merest mention of hard work," he said.

Suku tugged at Veera's sleeve. "Accept the challenge," he said. "We'll figure it out."

"Fine!" said Prince Veera. "Suku and I will count the crows by nightfall tomorrow."

King Bheema sat with his head in his hands. Maybe a holiday for the boys would have been better, he thought.

Suku stayed over at the palace that night and the boys kept busy trying to figure out how to count the crows.

"What about counting the crows in the garden and then multiplying that by the number of gardens in the city?" asked Veera.

"Maybe we could go for a walk in the morning and count all the crows we see," suggested Suku.

None of these ideas sounded right. They

could never count all the crows in a month, let alone one day.

"Perhaps we could tie a royal sign to all the crows we count," said Veera.

Suku started to giggle. "Imagine us running behind crows and getting pecked," he said. "The guards would be chasing the crows too. And then the crows would poop on us."

"Even if we did that," said Veera, "there would be a problem. What if a crow without a royal sign came into the royal garden?"

"We would tell Raja Apoorva that this is a crow coming from another city," said Suku.

Veera's eyes sparkled. Suku had saved the day again. He hugged Suku and danced around the room.

"Are you going to tell me what's made you so happy?"

"I've a plan to outwit Grand-uncle Apoorva and it is all because of your genius."

"How?"

"You'll find out soon enough," said Veera. That night he slept dreaming of crows pooping on Raja Apoorva.

The next morning, Veera and Suku went into town. After a long day strolling in the market, eating mangoes and drinking lassi, they returned home just in time for the meeting with the kings.

"You are both covered in dust," said King Bheema.

"We've been busy counting crows," replied Prince Veera.

"Really?" said Raja Apoorva. "So did you manage to count all of them?"

"We never fail," said Prince Veera. "Suku will now read out the number."

Even King Bheema was curious. How did the boys manage it?

Suku pulled out a parchment from his pocket.

"Drum rolls, please," said Prince Veera, smiling at Suku.

"We counted the crows in the gardens and markets, groves and swamps, and even the fields where the corn is being harvested," said Suku. "There are 75,325 crows in our capital city."

King Bheema wasn't sure whether to believe it or not. But Raja Apoorva was intrigued. How did they do it? Surely the number was wrong, he thought.

"What if I counted them and found more than 75,325 crows?"

"We knew you would ask that," said Prince Veera. "Crows are a very friendly species. Relatives and friends from other cities and kingdoms visit our crows. But to keep the counting accurate, we didn't count the visiting crows."

"You should reward them for their efforts," said King Bheema.

"Wait, wait," said Raja Apoorva. "One more question. What if I counted and there were fewer crows than the number you read out?"

"Your Majesty," said Suku. "The crows in our capital city have families far and wide in the kingdom. Some of them must have gone visiting."

King Bheema burst out laughing. "I hereby decree that the number of crows in our city is not excessive and there is no need to cull," he announced.

Raja Apoorva scowled, just for a second.

He realized that the two boys had beaten him at his own challenge.

Raja Apoorva clapped his hands and his guard brought a bag of gifts for the boys. "Well deserved," said the king. "May you rule with wisdom always."

A few weeks later, summer was nearing its end. The monsoon season was not far away. The winds had turned strong and cold. The visiting king was due to leave in a couple of days. As a farewell gesture, King Bheema invited his uncle to grace the royal court. Raja Apoorva readily agreed.

Prince Veera and Suku had been invited to attend too. Raja Apoorva watched the proceedings with great interest.

That afternoon, a poor man was brought before the king.

"My name is Omkar, Your Highness," said the man. "I never learned a trade or a skill and I didn't go to school. Now I'm unable to find a job so that I can feed my family."

King Bheema cleared his throat. But Raja Apoorva spoke first. "Dear nephew, Bheema," he said. "Would you allow me to hear this case?"

King Bheema hesitated for a moment and then nodded. "Of course," he said. "We would be delighted."

Veera looked at Suku and mouthed, "This is not good." But what could he do? His father had to respect the wishes of his uncle. That was an unwritten rule for all nephews.

Raja Apoorva wasted no time. He addressed the poor man in front of him. "Dear man, Omkar," he said. "What would you do to earn money for your family?"

"Anything, Your Highness," said Omkar.

"How about an unpleasant job?"

"Nothing is more unpleasant for me than to listen to my baby crying with hunger, Your Majesty," said Omkar. "I'm prepared to do anything."

"How do I know you're not just saying that?" asked Raja Apoorva. "I wish to test your words."

"I'll do anything, Your Majesty," repeated Omkar.

The man's suffering moved Veera and Suku. Families should not go hungry. Many times people had come asking for money and King Bheema would send them to the stables or the kitchens or to the garden to get work. Perhaps Raja Apoorva would find the man a job that would provide him with a livelihood.

Raja Apoorva said, "This is what I want you to do. I want you to stand by the royal

lake all night wearing nothing except your
dhoti."

The courtiers
gasped. Summer
was retreating.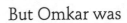
The night
would be chilly
and windy.

But Omkar was
desperate. He agreed to the king's test.

"If you succeed," said Raja Apoorva,
"I will take you with me to my kingdom
and give you a job in the palace."

The court was dismissed in silence.
Many people were worried for Omkar.
Prince Veera and Suku knocked on King
Bheema's door.

"Father, this is unfair," said Veera. "You've
got to do something about it."

"We cannot interfere," said King
Bheema. "Omkar agreed, didn't he? If he

had hesitated, I would have stepped in somehow."

"Your father is right," said Suku. "You've got to let Omkar prove to the world that he would do anything for his family."

"But if he dies?"

"The guards won't let that happen," said the king. "The royal doctor will be on hand."

Prince Veera wasn't convinced. But his father and Suku were right. They had to let Omkar try and win his fight with Grand-uncle, just as his father had let them count the crows.

That night, the boys watched from the palace windows. Omkar arrived with no shirt and no coat. He was wearing just a tattered dhoti. He stood on the banks of the lake, watched by two guards.

The moon climbed the sky and the oil lamps in the corridors and rooms were blown out. The palace slowly went to sleep.

Omkar was shivering in the cold, but he was determined to survive the night. He tried to distract himself by counting the columns in the palace corridors. Then he counted the fireflies.

The poor man was so cold that he was shaking. He tried to keep warm by rubbing his hands. He moved up and down the garden path surrounding the lake. Nothing helped.

Omkar hugged himself tight and looked at the sky. Even the moon was reluctant to watch him suffer. It hid behind the clouds. It was dark except for the light that flickered on the palace tower.

Omkar fixed his sight on the lamp. He imagined the flickering flame to be a raging fire. He imagined sitting before the fire and warming himself. He imagined roasting corn for his children.

As the guards rubbed their hands in the cold, Omkar was smiling. He was lost in his own imagination. He forgot about the cold wind and the mist that fell around him. All he could think about was the flame on top of the tower.

Slowly the moon moved away and let the sun return. At the crack of dawn, the guards took Omkar to the kitchen and gave him a warm drink and a blanket.

Soon it was time to go to the court. Omkar was confident that the king would give him a job and his family's suffering would be over. He was smiling even though he was still shaking from the cold. The courtiers had gathered early. Prince Veera and Suku had taken their places too. Everyone eagerly awaited the kings' arrival.

Raja Apoorva was surprised to see Omkar in the court.

"So you didn't run away?" asked the king.

"Why would I, Maharaj?" asked Omkar. "I need the job."

"Did he have help to keep warm?" the king asked the guard.

"No, sir," said the guard. "He stood there all night in his dhoti with a smile on his face."

"Why were you smiling?" asked Raja Apoorva.

"I was gazing at the tower lamp, Your Majesty," said Omkar. "And imagined it to be a raging fire. In my imagination I was happily roasting corn in the fire for my children."

"Aha!" said Raja Apoorva. "You've had help. You were warmed by the tower lamp. You didn't complete this challenge as per the conditions I set out."

Omkar was stunned. How could the

tower lamp warm him? It was so far away.

King Bheema bristled in anger. He had assigned this case to his uncle and couldn't interfere without insulting him. But it troubled him that one of his own citizens was not getting a fair hearing in his court.

Prince Veera and Suku, too, were outraged. How could Raja Apoorva treat the man with such callousness? Whoever heard of a lamp so far up in the tower warming a man by the lake? They had to do something. King Bheema shook his head slightly, warning them not to challenge Raja Apoorva.

Omkar was sent away from the court with nothing. King Bheema retired to his chambers, sullen and angry. As soon as the court was adjourned, the boys left the palace too.

"What about Omkar?" asked Suku.

"I'm sure Father will help him after Grand-uncle has gone," said Veera.

"But we have to show Raja Apoorva that this is not fair," said Suku. "We cannot let him leave without a lesson."

"I agree," said Prince Veera. "I've been thinking the same thing."

That afternoon King Bheema didn't want to see Raja Apoorva. He wanted to eat with the boys. But the guards told him that Prince Veera was having lunch at Suku's house.

Raja Apoorva, too, was on his own. He gloated to his guards that he had saved himself a bundle of money because Omkar was a cheat. He was proud of his judgement, and proud that Prince Veera had learned a lesson in running a court.

It was the final evening of Raja Apoorva's visit. The kings met in the garden for a stroll.

"Where is Veera?" asked King Bheema.

"He hasn't returned from Suku's house, Your Majesty," said the guard.

"Why don't we go for a ride, Uncle?" asked King Bheema. "Veera must say goodbye to you."

"Why don't you summon him here?" asked Raja Apoorva.

"I thought you might like to see the city at night."

Raja Apoorva agreed and the kings set off towards Suku's house.

As they dismounted their horses, Suku's father came out to greet them. "Welcome, Your Highnesses," he said. "I welcome both of you."

"Where is Veera?" asked King Bheema. "I want to see him right now."

"He's been cooking lunch all day, Your Majesty," said Suku's father.

"Cooking all day?" asked Raja Apoorva. "It's almost nightfall now. What kind of food is so special that he must cook all day?"

"He's just cooking rice, Your Majesty," said Suku's father. "Do come in."

The kings were curious. Why was Prince Veera cooking in Suku's house when a big pot of rice was always ready in the royal kitchens?

When they entered the kitchen, Raja Apoorva burst out laughing.

A stove was lit on the floor. A pot hung from the ceiling, far away from the heat.

"What are you doing, dear prince?" asked Raja Apoorva. "Surely you know how to cook rice? If not, do come to my palace and I will teach you personally."

"But I've learned this from you," said Prince Veera.

Suku giggled.

Raja Apoorva wasn't smiling, however. "What do you mean?" he demanded.

"You're a great monarch, Your Majesty," said Prince Veera. "For you even a tower lamp could warm a man by the lakeside. But I'm just a prince. I thought the blazing fire in the stove would heat the pot hanging just above it. That's not too much to ask, is it?"

King Bheema chuckled.

Raja Apoorva understood the prince's subtle message. The lamp in the tower was indeed too far away to warm the man by the lakeside. Omkar wasn't trying to cheat him. The poor man was desperate and he had been turned away.

"You're very wise," said Raja Apoorva. "I'm humbled by the lesson you've taught me. I was wrong to dismiss Omkar for imagining the warmth from the lamp."

King Bheema hugged Prince Veera and Suku. "I'm proud of you both," he said.

"I was so troubled by the judgement all day. You've indeed brought me joy."

That night Raja Apoorva summoned Omkar and his family. They were all fed and clothed and asked to accompany the king back to his kingdom. Omkar was given a job at Raja Apoorva's palace. Omkar and his family would never go hungry again.

"I bid you farewell, King Bheema," said Raja Apoorva. "You must bring your son and his friend to my palace next summer."

"As long as we don't have to count crows or cook rice," said Prince Veera, "we'd be delighted."

What's Fair?

It was a busy morning for Suku. He had
agreed to help out in the fields before going
to his classes with Prince Veera.

Suku's cousins and some neighbours
were working alongside him. Everyone
usually joked and laughed as they worked.
Sometimes they sang too. But this morning
they were talking about the guard who
stood outside the king's court. Suku inched
closer to listen.

"He will take half of everything you would get," said one woman.

"Really? Does the king know?" asked the other.

"No one dares to complain about the king's guard to the king," said the first woman.

"How do you know it's true?" asked the second.

"My brother went to see the king and was given ten silver pieces to build a new hut," said the first woman. "The guard took five of those. My brother has hardly anything left to finish the hut now."

"That's terrible," said the second woman.

Suku agreed. It was terrible. How could a king's guard be dishonest and corrupt? He had to tell Veera at once.

That day, after classes, as they munched on spicy puffed rice, Suku told Veera about the conversation he had overheard. Veera, too, was upset. It was his father's court, after all. He had to do something about it.

"That's the new guard," said Veera. "He was appointed only a few days ago."

"New or old," said Suku, "he's not supposed to take anything from the people."

"Maybe we should tell Father," said Veera.

"We've no proof," said Suku.

"Then what should we do?" asked Veera. "We need to put this right."

"Maybe we should catch him red-handed." Suku paused and thought for a moment. "I've a plan."

Veera listened as Suku outlined his idea. "That might work," said Veera. "Let's hope Father doesn't give the game away."

Veera quickly changed out of his expensive clothes and put on ordinary ones. He did this often when he and Suku visited markets and the village square. This time they were going to the royal court, pretending to be poor.

At the entrance there was a queue. They watched the guard as he talked to each person before they entered the big hall where the court was held.

"Do you think he's discussing his share?" asked Veera.

"Maybe," said Suku. "Or talking about the weather."

Veera chuckled. "For his sake, let's hope it is the weather."

The queue moved slowly. Finally it was Veera's turn.

"What do you want?" asked the guard. He hadn't recognized the prince and he didn't know Suku.

"We've come to see the king regarding a job," said Suku.

"If you want me to let you in," said the guard, "you must promise to give me half of what the king gives you."

"But..." said Veera. "That's unfair."

"Standing here all day is unfair," said the guard. "You give me my share or I won't let you in."

"Please let us in," said Suku. "We promise to give you half of everything we get."

"Clever boy," said the guard as he opened the door.

King Bheema sat up in his throne in surprise when he saw Veera and Suku enter. But he didn't say anything. Veera always had a reason for doing the things he did.

"State your case," said the usher.

"Your Majesty," said Veera, "we want to learn horse riding and become soldiers. But we cannot afford to pay for riding lessons."

Veera could ride like the wind and so could Suku, thought the king. What were the boys playing at?

"We want to train in your stables, Your Majesty," said Suku.

"You want to train at the royal stables?" asked the king, playing along. "My stable is not a free school."

"But we don't have any money," said Veera. "And no one else would teach us."

"Nothing comes for free," said the king. "If you want to train in the stables, first you have to prove worthy of it."

"We'll do anything, Your Majesty," said Suku.

"You must work hard collecting the dung

and cleaning the stables," said the king. "Then I'll let you train with my men."

"That's so kind of you, Your Majesty," said Veera. "There is just one more request."

"What's that?" asked the king. This was getting stranger by the minute.

"You have to let your guard come with us too," said Veera.

"Why?"

"We promised to give him half of everything we got, Your Highness," said Suku. "It's only fair that he, too, cleans the stables and be trained with us."

"Why would you do that?" asked the king.

"If we didn't promise him half of what we got from you," said Veera, "the guard wouldn't let us in, Your Majesty."

"Summon the guard!" shouted King Bheema to his minister. How dare someone demand a bribe for letting people into the court?

The guard was brought before the king.

"Thank you, Veera and Suku," said the king. "You've indeed saved me from disgrace."

The court cheered the boys, crying "Long live Prince Veera! Long live Suku!"

The guard realized his greed had landed him in big trouble. As he was new, he had not recognized the prince and his friend. The king decreed that the guard would be sent to work in the stables. Stripped of his guard duty and all of his ill-gotten wealth, the guard would have to collect horse dung for a long time.

"It's good of you to take the farm gossip seriously," said Suku.

Veera shrugged. "Listening to what everyone says is part of the job," he said. "But now I want to play in the streets with you."

Suku was the king of street-games – especially *gilli-danda* – the game of stick and stone. The boys set off to play near Suku's house. They rode their horses through the market square and past the village temple.

64

As always Veera's guards followed him at a discreet distance.

"Wait!" called out Suku.

"What?"

"Someone is sleeping on the temple steps," said Suku.

"He must be waiting for the temple to open," said Veera.

"I want to check," said Suku. "Maybe he's hungry or lost."

Veera followed him. The man had a tattered shawl draped over him and a dirty yellow cloth bag under his head.

"I think he's homeless," said Suku.

"But..." Veera hesitated. "I thought we provided homes to all homeless people."

"Perhaps he has come from another town, looking for work."

"Wake him up," said Veera. "Let's get him to a *choultry* – all travellers get food and shelter there, don't they?"

The guards woke the sleeping man.
As soon as he opened his eyes and saw the
guards, he tried to bolt.

"Don't be afraid," said Prince Veera.
"We mean no harm. We just want to help."

"No one can help me," said the man,
covering his face with a towel. "Please let
me go."

Prince Veera gestured to his guards to wait
on the street.

"Now that it's just the two of us boys,"
said Suku, "tell us why you're sleeping on
the temple steps."

"My name is Kalu," said the man. "I've
been running from one place to another ever
since I escaped."

"Escaped from where?" asked Veera.

"From Sheetalpur," said Kalu. "From King Athi's men."

"Why?" asked Suku. "Did you commit any crime?"

"My crime was my tickly nose," said Kalu. "All I did was sneeze at the wrong time."

Prince Veera was intrigued. What was this man's problem? How could a sneeze incur the wrath of King Athi?

Suku signalled to Veera to step aside.

"If he's running away from a royal punishment," said Suku, "your duty is to return him to King Athi of Sheetalpur."

"But—"

"King Athi could invade your kingdom if you give shelter to one of his prisoners," said Suku.

"But—"

"Veera, this is not gilli-danda," warned Suku. "You have to follow the royal charters of all the kingdoms around you. Otherwise you'll put your own kingdom in danger."

But Veera wanted to find out more. How could sneezing be a crime?

"My dear Kalu," said Veera. "Tell us what happened."

"I worked for King Athi, looking after his royal attire and his chambers," explained Kalu. "We were all invited to his wedding."

"Did you steal anything?" asked Suku.

"Of course not," said Kalu. "I did the one thing that King Athi couldn't forgive."

"Did you eat his wedding cake?"

Kalu smiled sadly. "Maybe even that would not have caused my troubles," he said. "I sneezed just at the moment King Athi tied the sacred knot of marriage."

"What?" Suku gasped. "That was so inauspicious."

"Of course it was," said Kalu. "At least for me. King Athi thought it signalled an unhappy marriage and ordered his men to put me to death."

Veera bristled with anger. "No one should be put to death for sneezing," he said. "That's not fair."

"Didn't anyone try to help you?" asked Suku. He felt the same way as Veera, now that he had heard the man's story. How could they send him back to King Athi, who had been so rash and selfish?

"The new queen intervened," said Kalu. "She begged for mercy."

"Did that work?" asked Veera.

"A little," said Kalu. "The king allowed me to choose how I wanted to die. But die I must, he said."

"That's terrible," said Veera.

"I escaped from the wedding hall," said Kalu. "And I've been running ever since."

"Maybe King Athi will have cooled down by now?" asked Suku.

"No chance of that," said the man, showing a parchment with his name and a reward for catching him written on it.

Suku and Veera sat down on the temple steps. They had to send the man back to Sheetalpur. But they didn't want him to be put to death either. Was there another way?

"Maybe he should choose poison," said Suku. "That would be quick."

"You're not helping," said Veera.

"Maybe he should be trampled by an elephant?" asked Suku.

"Don't be like that," said Veera.

"Maybe every day for a month he could read the stories you write," said Suku. "That would kill him for sure."

"Very funny," said Veera. "Maybe he could read your poems. That would kill him instantly."

"It hasn't killed you," said Suku.

"That's because I've become immune to them," said Veera. At that moment, something clicked in his head.

"Maybe—" began Suku.

"Wait a moment," said Veera. "I think I've found a way to save Kalu."

"What's that?" asked Suku.

"Kalu, you could die of old age," said Veera. "That would satisfy the king's decree and let you live until you are old."

Kalu's eyes lit up. That was perfect. The boys had saved his life.

"You're a genius," said Suku. "But he

should stop going to weddings or sneezing, or both, until he's really old."

Veera instructed his guards to take Kalu back to Sheetalpur. Kalu was confident of escaping King Athi's wrath and relieved to be going back home to see his family.

"Now, it's time I beat you at gilli-danda," said Suku.

"I may beat you today," said Veera.

"Not a chance – not even when you're old and wrinkled," said Suku, riding ahead.

Grey Elephants
and Five Fools

Suku's aunt Chandra was a washerwoman. While she worked, she sang songs about the forests and the trees, the rivers and the bees. People in the village often stopped outside her house to listen. Like all washerwomen, she had a donkey.

73

The donkey carried her load to and from the river and sang with her whenever it pleased. But of course the donkey's braying was not sweet, like Chandra's voice. Like any other donkey, its braying was loud and harsh.

One evening, Suku saw his aunt Chandra in the market.

"Hello, Aunt Chandra," said Suku. "How are you today?"

"Same old, same old," said Chandra. "Every day I get into a fight with the potter next door."

"Why?" asked Suku.

"The potter gets upset about everything I do: 'You beat your clothes too loudly,' he says. 'Your donkey brays too loudly; your singing is horrible.'"

"But you sing beautifully," said Suku. "That man must have no taste."

"Mark my words, nephew," said Chandra, "one day that potter is going to bring a bundle of trouble and drop it on my doorstep."

"I hope that doesn't happen," said Suku. "But if it does, I'll be there to help you."

One day, the potter was working on a vase for a rich man. It was a special order worth a lot of money. The potter had spent hours preparing the clay and setting it up on his potter's wheel. He didn't want anything to go wrong.

The clay was poised on the wheel as it began to spin. Slowly, the vase began to take shape in the potter's deft hands. Just when he was curving his fingers to shape the neck of the vase, he heard *"Hee haw! Hee haw!"*

The potter was so startled that he let go of the vase. Now it lay splattered on the ground in a big lump. He would have to start all over again. The potter was enraged at the donkey and the washerwoman, who had allowed the donkey to sing. "No one should encourage donkeys to sing," he mumbled. "Enough is enough. I'm going to get rid of the woman and her donkey once and for all."

That night he lay awake plotting an evil plan.

Early the next morning, the potter stood in the queue to meet King Bheema.

"What can I do for you?" asked the king.

"I have not come to ask for help, Your Majesty," said the potter. "I have come to help *you*."

The king was astonished. How could the man possibly help him? Was he a spy? A wise man with advice? Or an astrologer with a prediction for the forthcoming year?

"Do tell me," said King Bheema. "I'm intrigued."

"I'm a potter, Your Majesty," said the man. "I saw Airavata, the celestial elephant that

belongs to Indra, the god of
thunder, in my dreams."

"I hear that's a good
omen," said the king, still
unsure why the man was
in his court.

"Yes, Your Majesty," said the
potter. "But I wondered why that
dream came to me. That's when I realized
it wasn't for me. I don't have any elephants.
The gods were sending a message to you
through me."

"And what message would that be?"
asked the king.

"Even though your royal elephants are tall
and strong," said the potter, "they are still as
grey as the monsoon clouds."

The king wasn't sure if the man was mad
or genuinely trying to help. He decided to
listen to him – after all, that's why he kept
the doors to his court open.

"What should I do?" asked King Bheema.

"I know someone who can wash your elephants and turn them as white as Airavata," said the potter.

"Really?" said the king. "Who is that?"

"My neighbour, the washerwoman Chandra," said the potter. "She could turn even the greyest of clothes white. She would be perfect for the job."

The king was amused. Who was this miracle woman who could turn his elephants from grey to white? Was the potter trying to get a job at the palace for his neighbour?

"Bring the washerwoman to my court tomorrow," ordered the king.

When the news spread about the potter's dream and his suggestion to the king, everyone was afraid for Chandra. How could she change the colour of the elephants?

Soon the rumours reached Chandra too.

She was worried. She had known the day would come when the potter would bring her harm. What was she going to do? Maybe Suku could help, she thought. Suku visited the king often and was friends with the prince. Maybe Suku could tell the king about the potter's ploy.

Chandra went to Suku's house and explained the situation. "Tell me how to get out of this," she begged.

"Don't worry, Aunt Chandra," said Suku. "I'll come up with something."

Suku didn't waste a moment. He set off to the palace to see Prince Veera.

"I need your help, my friend," said Suku. He told Veera about the tiff between the potter and his aunt and how it had reached the palace.

"I don't like this at all," said Veera. "It is one thing to have a disagreement with a neighbour; everyone does."

"We have seen so many cases of that," agreed Suku. He recalled the neighbours fighting about wells and water, mango pickles and precious gems.

"But to bring it to the king and make him party to their feud," said Prince Veera, "well, that's crossing the line."

"And she is my aunt," said Suku. "I need to help her."

"I'm sure Father will be fair," said Veera. "We should teach the potter a lesson, though."

Suku agreed. They couldn't just complain about the potter to the king. They needed a plan.

"Can you show me how your aunt washes clothes?" said Veera.

"Like everyone else, I suppose," said Suku.

"I have never washed my own clothes," said Veera. "So show me."

Suku took Veera back to his aunt's house

80

in the village. She had bundles of dirty clothing to wash.

"I soak the clothes in big pots, like this," explained Chandra. "Then I beat them on a stone. After that I wash them in the river and dry them on the riverbank."

Veera watched with fascination. He should learn about all the trades in his kingdom, he thought. Now every time he put on clean clothes, he would appreciate the work that went into washing them.

"What if you had to wash a big blanket?" asked Veera.

"I would need a bigger pot," said Chandra. "I would get one from the market. The potter next door has a shop there."

Veera smiled. "I think I know how to outwit the potter," he said. "But you must do what I tell you." Then Veera explained his plan to Suku and Chandra.

That night Chandra slept peacefully. She knew the prince's idea would save her from the wrath of the king and perhaps even stop the potter from bothering her again.

Early the next morning, the king summoned the washerwoman to the court. Prince Veera and Suku were there too.

"I order you to wash my elephants and turn them white, just like Airavata, the celestial elephant in the skies," said King

Bheema. He was sure the woman would refuse. Who could do such a task?

The washerwoman didn't seem perturbed at all. She smiled at the king and said, "Of course, Your Majesty. May I see your elephants first?"

The king was taken aback.

"Perhaps we should invite the potter too, to come with us to the stables," said Prince Veera. "After all, it was his dream."

The king agreed, and the potter was summoned. When he arrived, he joined the king and his entourage as they walked to the stables with Chandra, Veera and Suku.

Chandra entered the stables. She walked around the first elephant. She took out a string and measured the elephant. She touched its back and its trunk. Then she repeated the same process with the second elephant. She pursed her lips, nodded and muttered to herself.

 The king
watched with
amusement as
she considered
the task. Suku
and Veera
were watching
the potter. He looked
far more afraid than the washerwoman.

Finally, after a few minutes of inspection,
Chandra stepped out of the stables. She
looked at the king solemnly and said, "I
think I can wash these elephants and turn
them white, Your Majesty."

"What?" the king exclaimed in surprise.

"But I need a few supplies before I can get
to work."

"What do you need?" asked Veera.

"I need two pots to soak each of
these elephants," she said. "The pots
need to be big and strong enough

to hold the elephants overnight."

The king caught on quickly. He looked at Veera and Suku, who were grinning from ear to ear.

The king turned to the potter and said, "Dear man, your idea was wonderful. Now I am relying on you to make the biggest, strongest pots to soak my elephants in."

The potter gasped. His mouth fell open in shock. "B-but..." he stammered.

"Come with the pots," said the king, "as soon as you can."

The potter ran from the stables back to his house. He packed his bags and left the village, lest the king should send soldiers asking for the pots.

Chandra left the palace happy. She had managed to thwart the potter's ploy.

"So tell me, boys," said the king. "Did the washerwoman have any help?"

Suku nodded and pointed at Veera. "She is

my aunt, Your Majesty," he said. "And I'm grateful to Veera for helping me."

"I knew it," said the king. "Well done!"

That night the village celebrated the potter's defeat and Chandra's victory with a big feast. The guests of honour were Prince Veera and his best friend, Suku.

A few days later, a poet was invited to the king's court. It was customary for visiting

poets to recite some
verses in honour of the
king and his kingdom.
The king would then reward the
poet with money and perhaps even
a title.

The poet spent the whole morning
reciting poems about the king's generosity.
The king rewarded him with a lavish
lunch with himself and his courtiers. In the
afternoon, the poet recited poems about
how the kingdom was filled with clever
people. He read out many verses exalting
the wisdom of not just the king and his
court, but every citizen in the kingdom.

Prince Veera and Suku listened to the last
few verses from the balcony upstairs. "The
poet is very talented," said Suku.

"He exaggerates," said Prince Veera. "He's
just trying to impress Father."

"It's not so easy to impress you," said Suku.

That evening, after the poet had set off on his journey with a cart full of gifts, the king was in a good mood.

"I agree with the poet," said the king. "Our kingdom is filled with wise men and women. We have no fools."

Prince Veera nudged Suku. "I told you," he whispered. "The poet has given Father a high horse."

"What horse?" asked King Bheema, catching the last word in Veera's sentence.

"You shouldn't believe everything the poet said, Father," said Veera. "He used the word *wise* just to rhyme with *nice*."

"I'm not that naïve," said the king. "I sincerely believe I don't have any fools in my kingdom."

"What if I prove you wrong?" said Veera. "Suku and I will make our way through the village and find five fools. We'll meet you at the palace gardens in an hour."

The king smiled. "You're bored, I think," he said. "I challenge you to find a single fool, let alone five."

Veera and Suku set off towards the village. On their way, they met a woman who was searching for something in the river.

"What are you looking for?" asked Suku.

"My gold ring," said the woman.

"When did you lose it?" asked Suku.

"This afternoon, when I was working."

"Where were you working?" asked Suku.

"In the mangrove," said the woman.

"Why are you looking in the river if you lost the ring in the mangrove?" asked Prince Veera.

"You're so silly," said the woman. She had not recognized the prince. "The mangrove is dark now. But the river is well lit. There's a better chance of finding the ring here."

"Come with me," said the prince. "We'll get someone to find your ring for you tomorrow."

So the woman followed the boys as they walked to the village.

On their way, they met a farmer on a donkey, with a bundle of firewood on his head. "Dear man," said Prince Veera, walking alongside the donkey. "Why don't you place the firewood on the donkey's back?"

The man was aghast at the suggestion.

"Can't you see my donkey is very tired?" asked the man. "How can I burden it with the firewood too?"

Prince Veera invited the man to join them. Suku offered to carry the firewood until they reached the palace.

As the party of four made their way through the village, they saw a man lying on his back in the street. His hands were up in the air and he was calling out to people to help him get up.

What is he doing? wondered Prince Veera.

Suku placed the bundle of firewood on the ground and asked the man about his predicament.

"Can't you see my hands are far apart?" answered the man. "How can I get up without moving them?"

"Why are you holding them apart?" asked Suku.

"Because that's the length of the fabric my wife asked me to bring from the shops."

"Why are you on the ground, then?" asked Prince Veera. "Surely the fabric shop is not down there?"

"I slipped on a banana peel and fell," said the man. "I can't get up without moving my hands. And if I move my hands, I'll forget the measurement."

Prince Veera and Suku helped the man up without holding his hands and asked that he, too, come with them.

"Our job is done here," said Veera. "Let's go to the palace."

"But..." said Suku. They had only three fools with them. Veera had promised the king he would find five.

"Trust me," said Veera.

Suku smiled. Veera must have something up his sleeve.

When they reached the palace, the king was strolling in the gardens impatiently.

"There you are," he said. "I'm sure you found no fools in my kingdom."

"I found five soon enough, Your Highness," said Veera.

The king looked at the woman who was crying for her ring, the farmer on the donkey and the man with his hands held far apart.

Veera explained why he had brought them.

"There are only three," said the king. "Have you failed?"

"You haven't counted all the fools," said Veera. "In addition to the three I brought, you already know the other two."

The king looked puzzled.

"The fourth fool is me, Your Majesty, for going on an errand to fetch fools," said Veera. "And the fifth fool is you, who got taken in by the words of the poet and believed that your kingdom could have no fools."

Suku gasped. Had Veera crossed the line? He had just called the king a fool!

The king was silent. The garden was quiet except for the call of the birds returning home to roost.

Suddenly the king erupted into laughter, startling the three people that Veera had brought to the palace. "You're right, as usual, my dear son," said the king. "I was blinded by the praise of the poet. I had forgotten that it takes all sorts to make a kingdom. We can't all be brave, wise and funny."

"Yes, Your Majesty," said Prince Veera. "No one is wiser than you."

That evening as they walked back to the palace, Prince Veera hoped that he, too, would be as humble and wise as his father and that his best friend, Suku, would be by his side to point out his faults without fear.

Chitra Soundar

is originally from the culturally colourful India, where traditions, festivals and mythology are a way of life. As a child, she feasted on generous portions of folktales and stories from Hindu mythology. As she grew older, she started making up her own stories. Chitra now lives in London, cramming her little flat with storybooks of all kinds.

Uma Krishnaswamy

has always loved the folk traditions of India and other cultures for the richness and vibrancy of colour, form and perspective. Coming from a culture that straddles modernity and tradition with ease, mixes regional and other flavours to spice things up, she works at reflecting these contradictory elements, hopefully with some degree of success. She also teaches Visual Studies in Chennai, where she lives.